MW01178459

This Ladybird Book belongs to:

_____

_____

_____

_____

Published by Penguin Books India
11 Community Centre, Panchsheel Park, New Delhi 110017

© PENGUIN BOOKS INDIA LTD 2005
5 7 9 10 8 6 4

ISBN 978-1-84422-738-9

Printed in Manipal Press Ltd., Manipal

FAVOURITE TALES

The Magic Mangoes

This Ladybird retelling by
MEERA UBEROI

illustrated by
UMA KRISHNASWAMY

based on a story from the Jataka Tales

A young man left his city to make his fortune. It was the middle of winter and very cold.

After many days of travelling, he found himself near a Chandala village. Now, Chandalas are tribal villagers, and many city people are scornful of them. As was our young man.

Standing in a mango grove outside the village, he thought, 'It will soon be dark. But how can I spend the night in a Chandala village?'

As he was about to walk on, a curious sight caught his eye, and he paused to look.

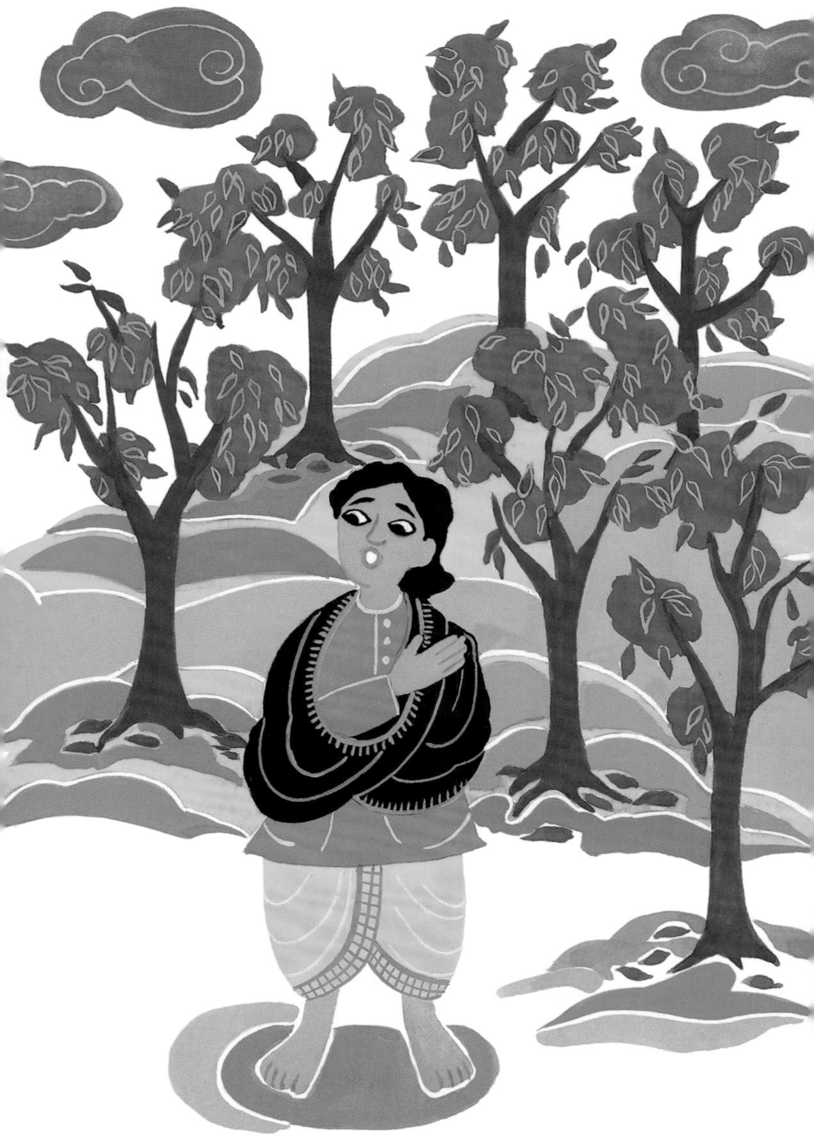

Standing under a bare mango tree was a sage with a long, curly beard. Murmuring some words, he sprinkled water on the tree trunk.

What happened next made the young man's eyes pop out and his jaw drop.

The tree began to sprout. In the blink of an eye, leaves covered all the branches and mango blossoms scented the air. Bees arrived and hummed as they flitted from flower to flower. A moment later, the flowers shed their petals and little green mangoes appeared. Another moment later, the tree was laden with juicy, golden mangoes.

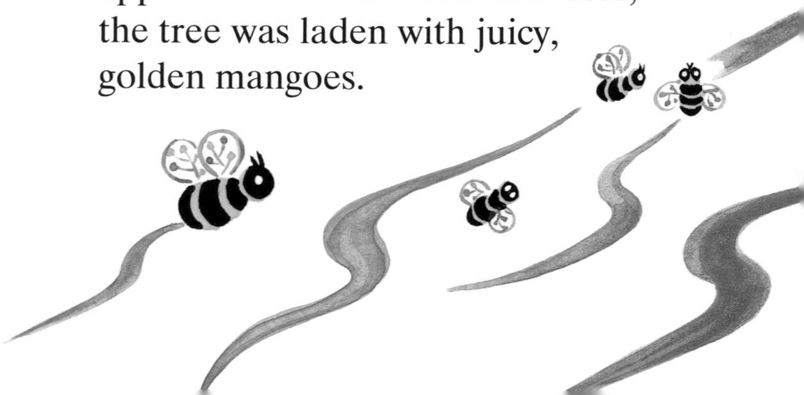

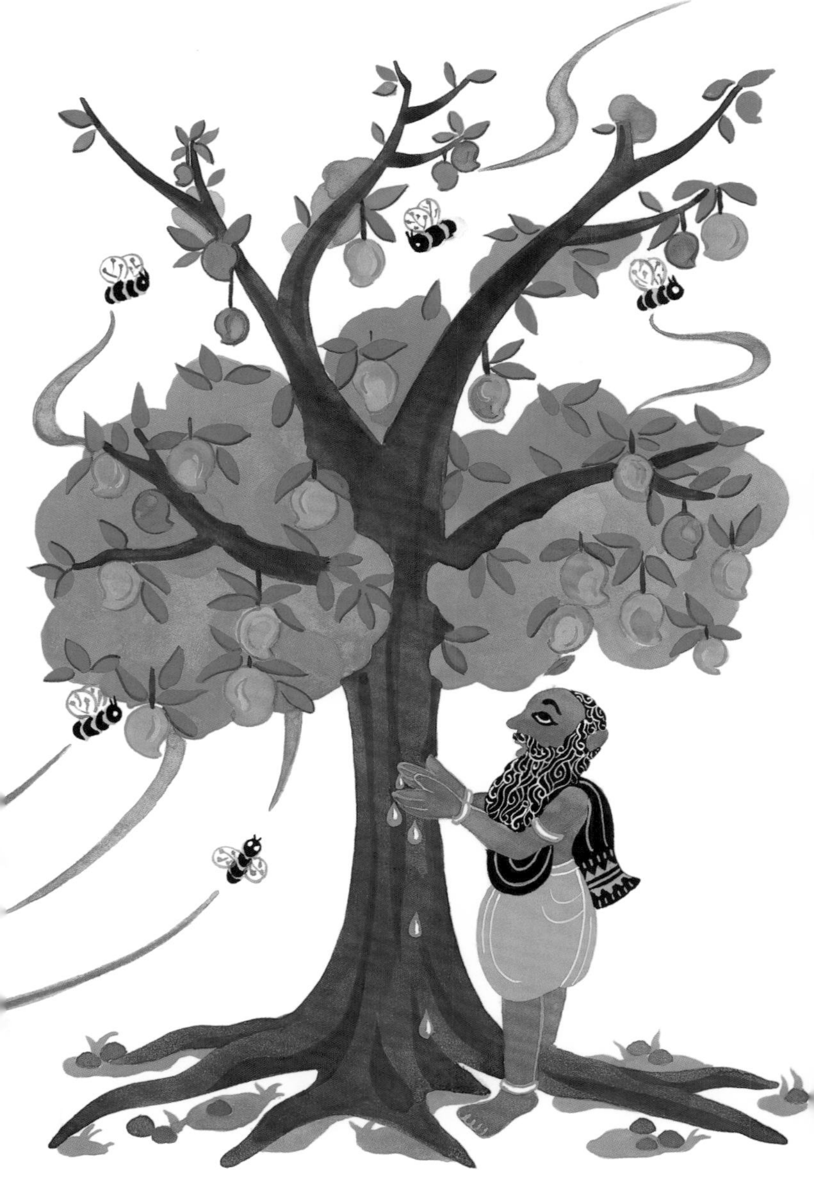

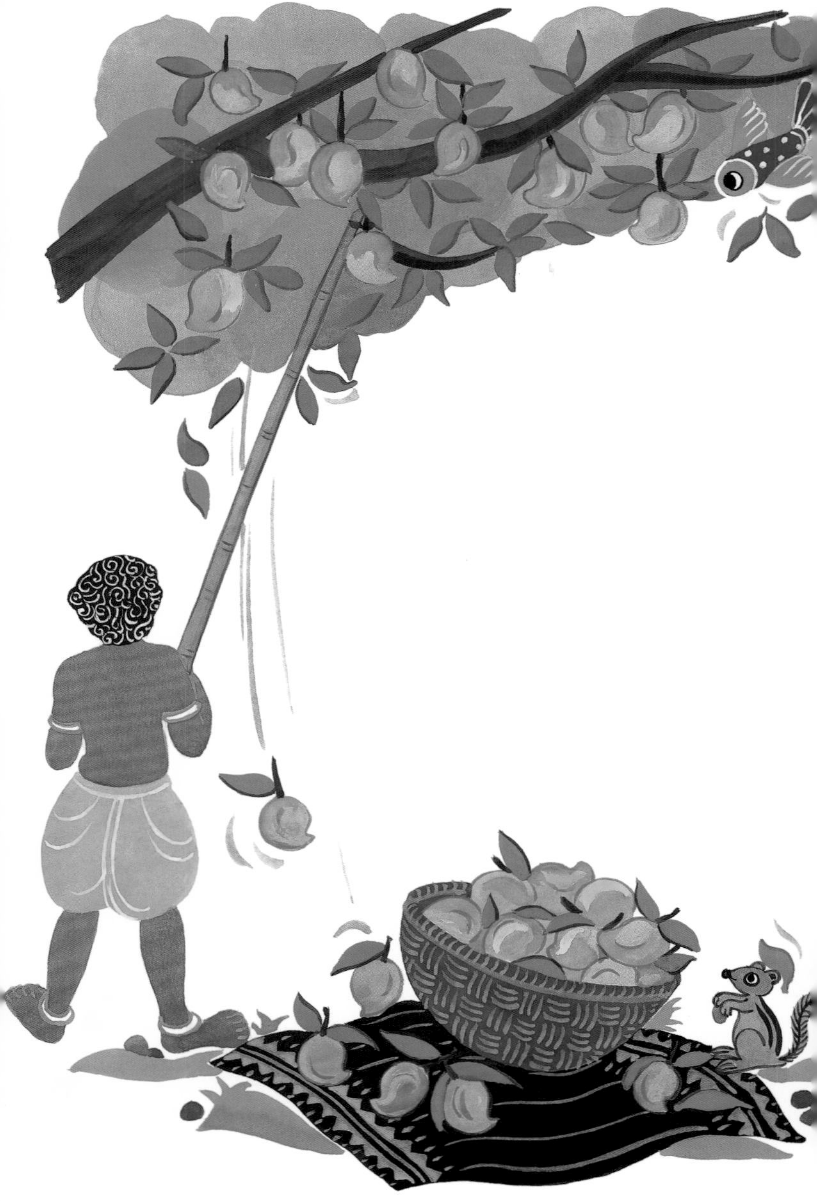

The young man rubbed his eyes. This couldn't be happening! Mangoes grew only in summer.

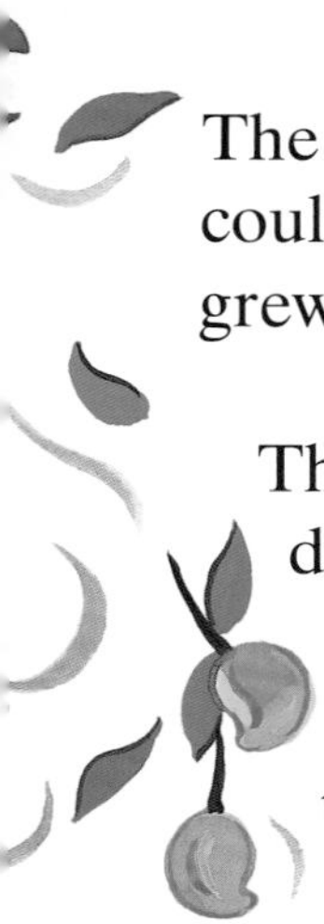

The sage knocked the mangoes down with a long pole. He gathered the fruit in a basket. As soon as he gathered all the fruit, the branches were bare once more.

'Wow!' breathed the young man softly. 'What a treasure that old man has!' The wonder in his eyes changed to cunning. 'This old man has a spell that gives him mangoes even in winter. With that spell, I can make a fortune!'

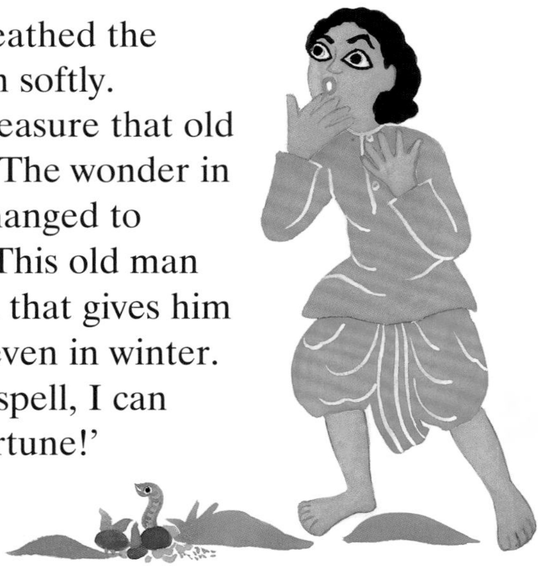

He ran after the old man. 'Great one, let me carry that basket for you,' he panted. 'It will be an honour to serve you. Make me your disciple!'

The sage gave the young man a sharp look as he handed him the basket. 'I am a villager. I can't read or write. Why would you want to be my disciple?'

The young man pleaded and begged.

When they reached the sage's house, the old man went in and said to his wife, 'This city lad wants to work with us. I don't think he should stay.'

The wife liked the look of the young man. 'He looks like a fine young man,' she said. 'You know we are getting old. It will be good to have a young man around the house.'

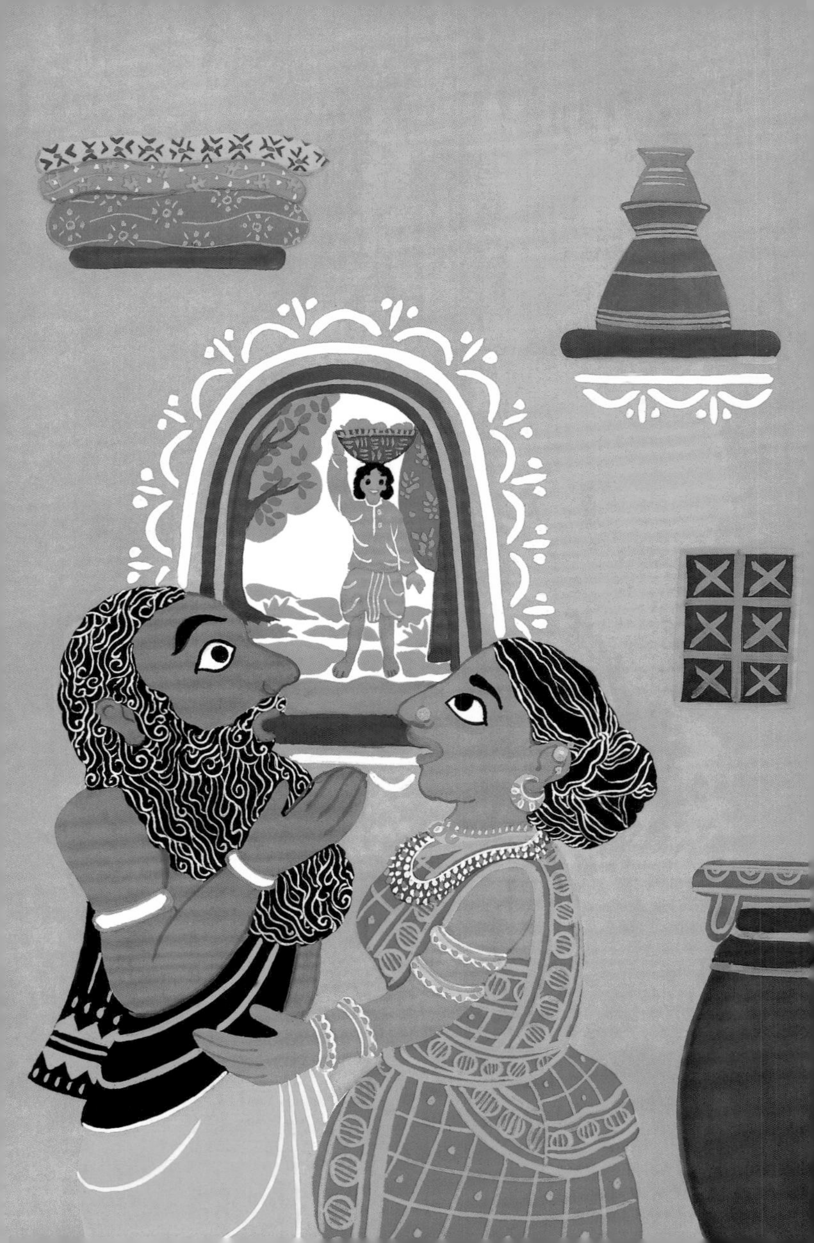

The old man shook his head.

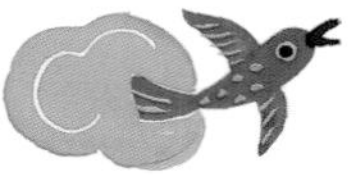

'He only wants my spell, that's why he wants to work for us, not because I am a worthy teacher. He does not look like a young man who wants my kind of wisdom.'

'Rubbish!' snapped his wife. 'He looks like a decent young man who will work hard and study well.'

'He looks good, but he isn't as good as he looks,' said the man. 'But since you wish it, he may stay.'

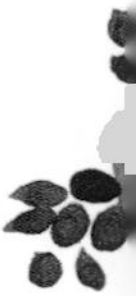

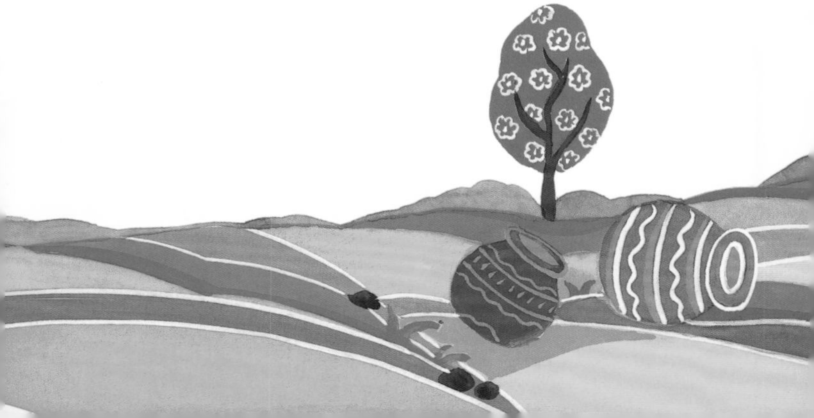

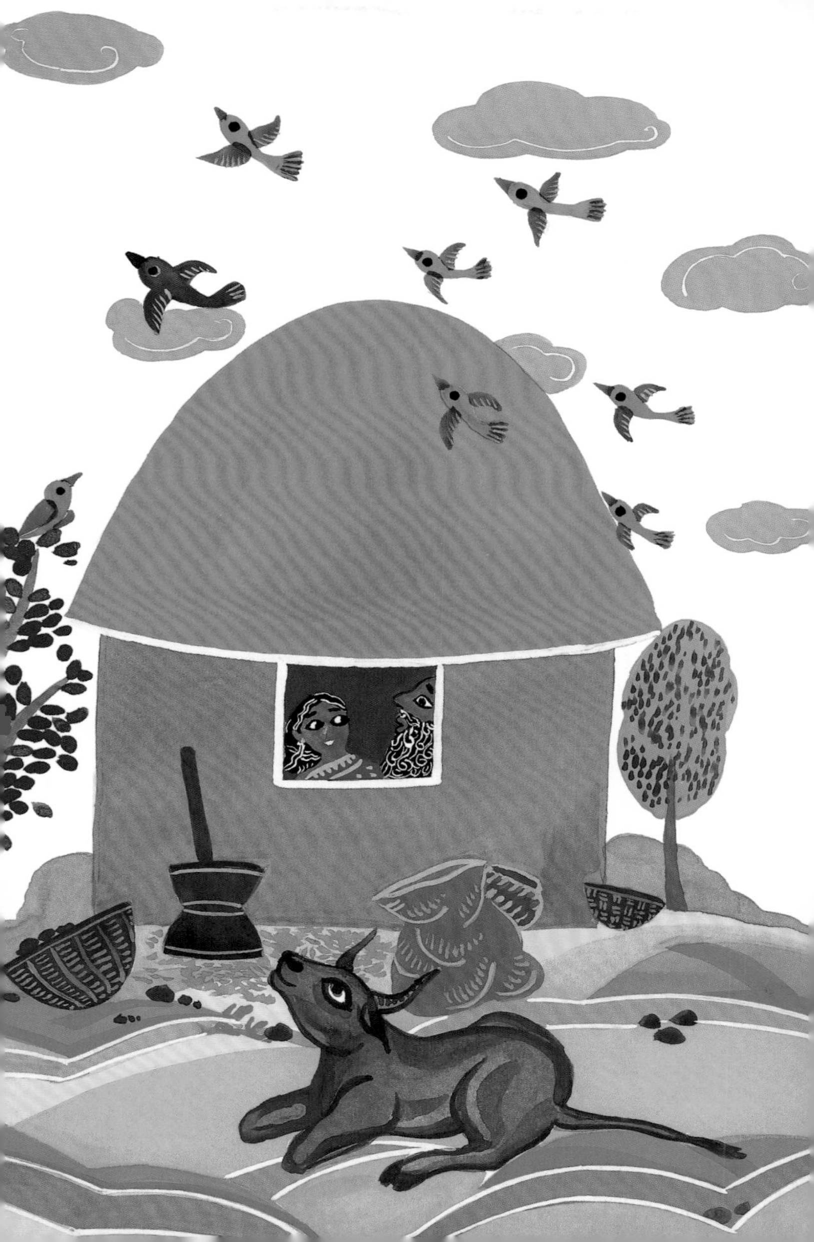

So the young man joined the household. He worked hard every day. Every night he would listen to the old sage's stories. He never complained or grumbled.

Months went by. The old man's wife was very pleased with the young man.

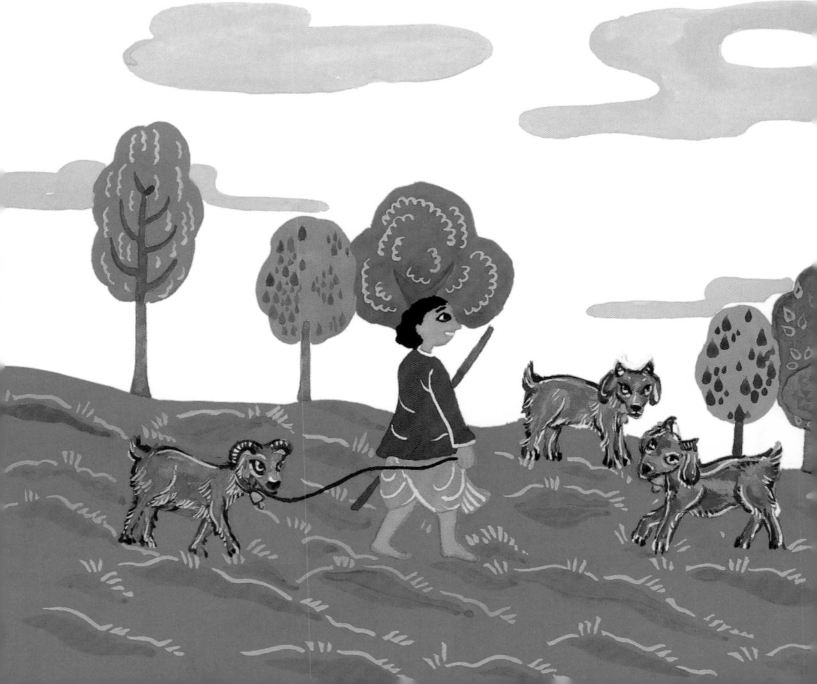

One day, she said to her husband, 'The young man has worked hard for a year and a half now. It's time you rewarded him.'

'I agree he has worked very hard,' said the old sage. 'But he has done so for the wrong reasons. Still, since you insist, I'll give him the magic spell.'

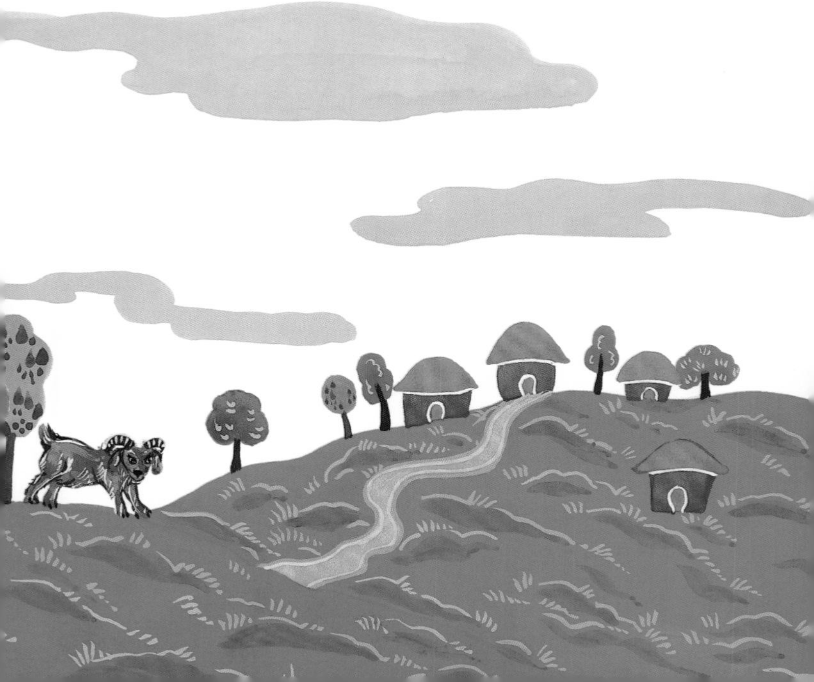

The next morning, he sent for the young man.

'Since you have worked so well, I am going to reward you with a priceless spell. It will bring you wealth and honour. But there is a condition. If anyone asks you who your teacher is, you must speak the truth. You must say that I, an illiterate villager, taught you all you know. If you are ashamed of me, if you lie, the spell will no longer work,' he said.

'I'll tell the world proudly that you were my teacher,' said the young man.

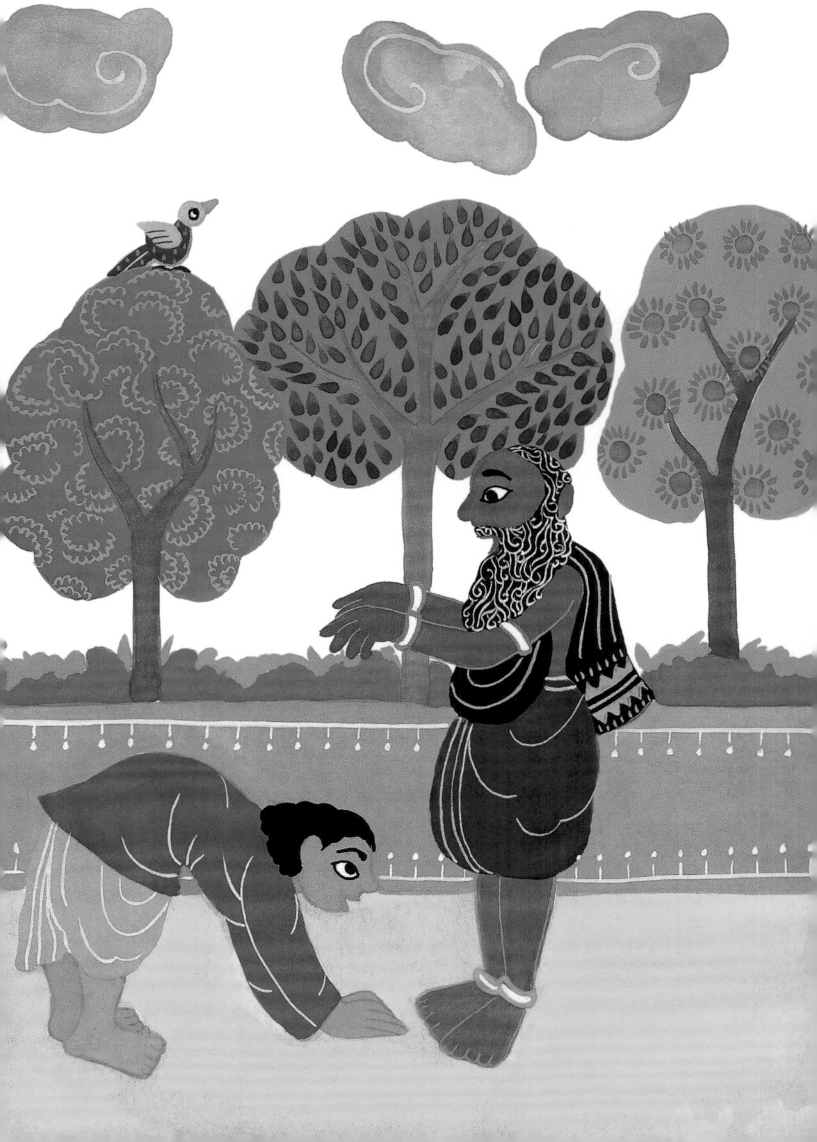

The old man taught him the spell. The young man left the village and went to Benaras.

In the city, he set up a stall in the market and began to sell mangoes. As summer ended, there were fewer and fewer mangoes in the market each week. But at that one stall, there were always lots of juicy, golden fruit.

One winter morning, the king of Benaras noticed to his great surprise that there were still mangoes on his table. 'Mangoes in December!' he exclaimed. 'Bring the mango-seller to me at once!'

The guards went to the market, found the young man and marched him back to the palace.

The king beamed with delight when he saw him. 'If you can get mangoes in winter, you should work for me!' he declared.

And so the young man began to work for the king. Very soon, he earned much wealth and honour.

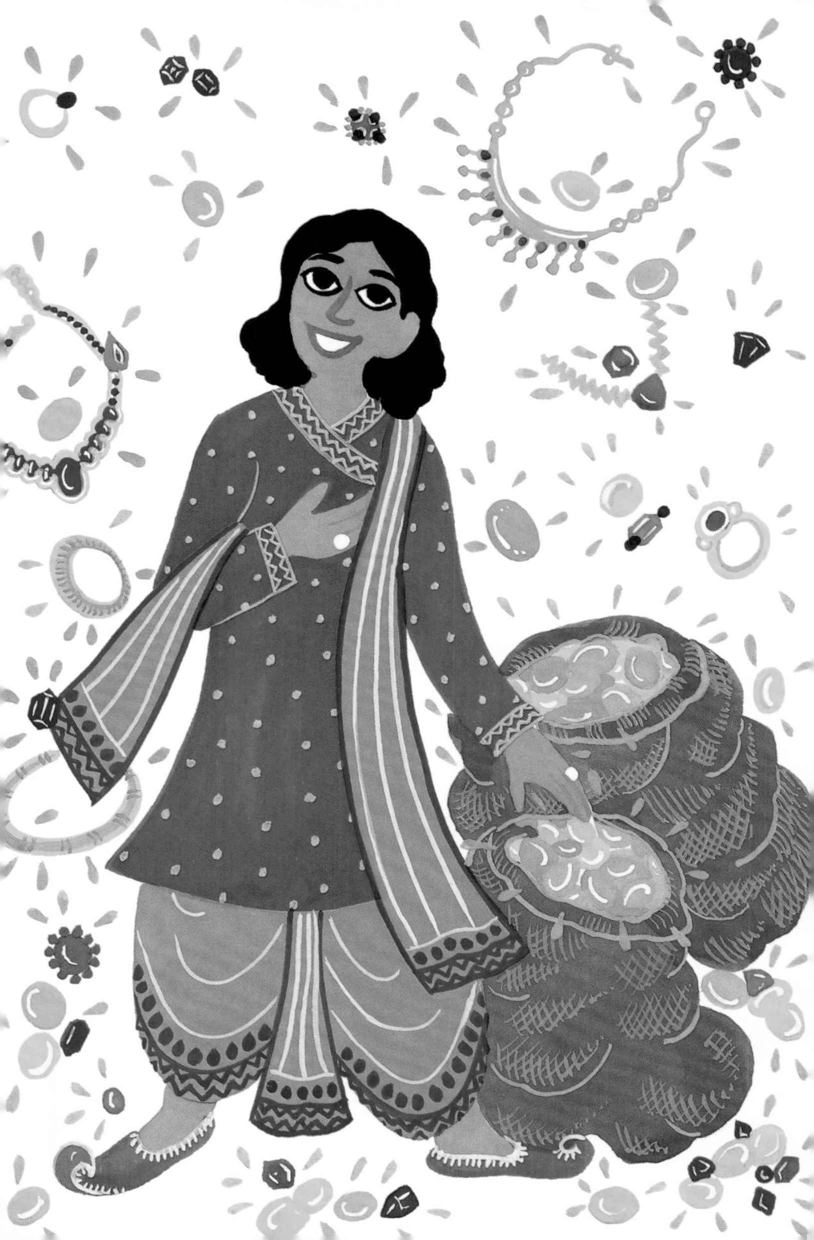

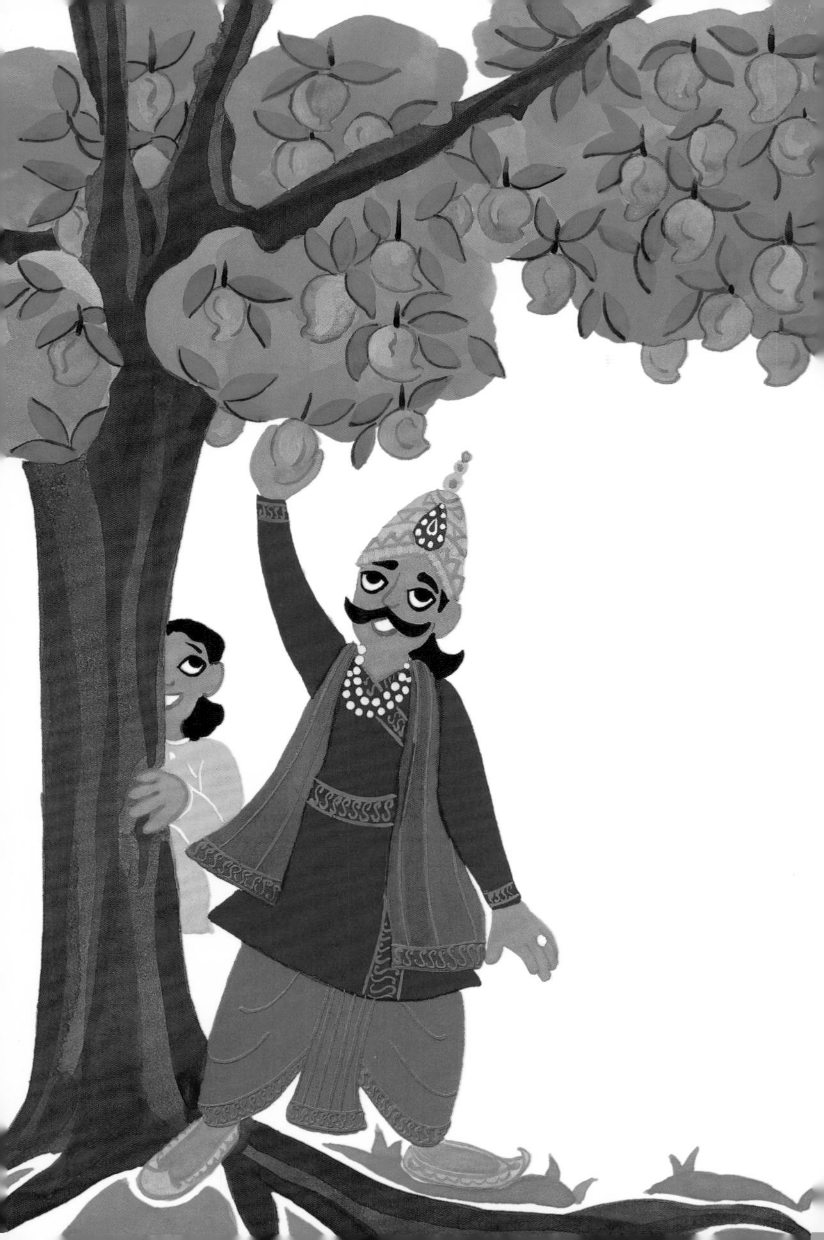

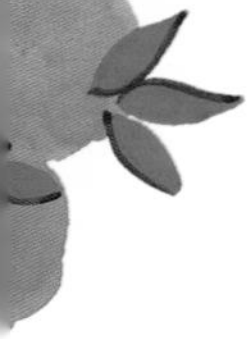

One day, the king asked the young man, ‘How do you get mangoes in winter?’

The young man told the king about the spell and showed him how it worked. The king was delighted and gave him a casket of jewels.

A few days later, the king asked, ‘Who taught you this wonderful spell?’

The young man went pale and still. ‘I’ll lose all my honour if I tell the king that my teacher was a tribal villager.’ So he decided to lie. ‘My teacher was a great sage,’ he told the king, ‘educated at world-famous universities.’

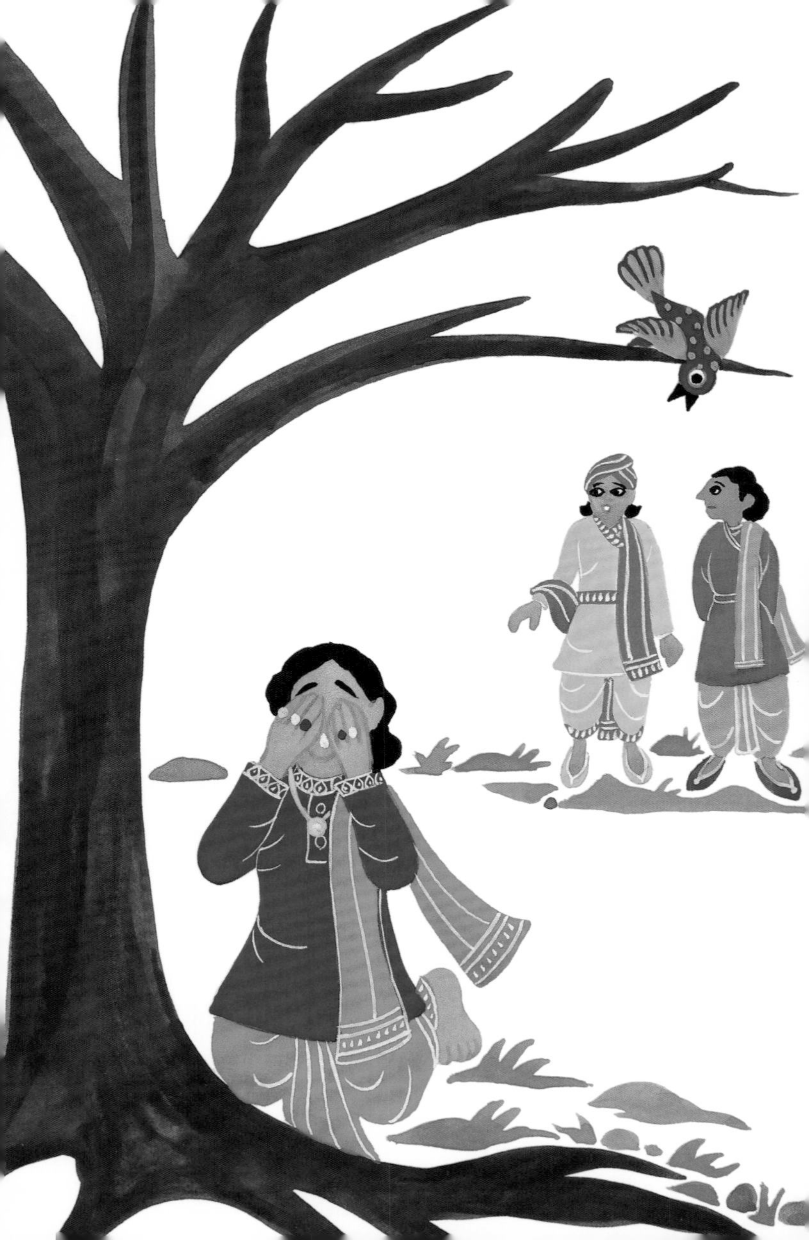

A few days later, the king asked for mangoes. The young man went to the grove. Murmuring the spell, he sprinkled water on the tree. To his horror, nothing happened. The tree remained bare.

Just then, the king arrived. 'Where are my mangoes?' he asked.

The young man hung his head in shame. 'It's gone,' he muttered.

'Gone! What do you mean?' snapped the king.

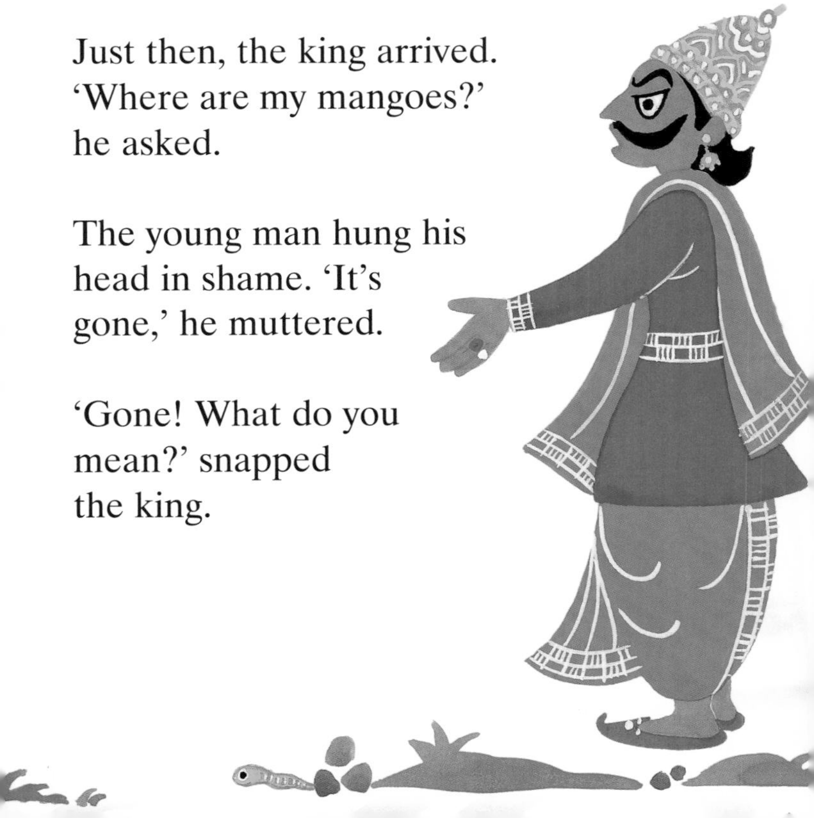

'The spell left me when I lied,' admitted the young man. 'I lied when I said my teacher was a famous sage. In fact, he was a man in a village. He warned me that this would happen if I lied.'

The king's face went cold. 'Famous university, illiterate villager, what does this matter? What is important is that a man is wise and good. You should be ashamed, not of him, but of yourself. There is no place in my court for the likes of you. Leave my kingdom and do not return!'

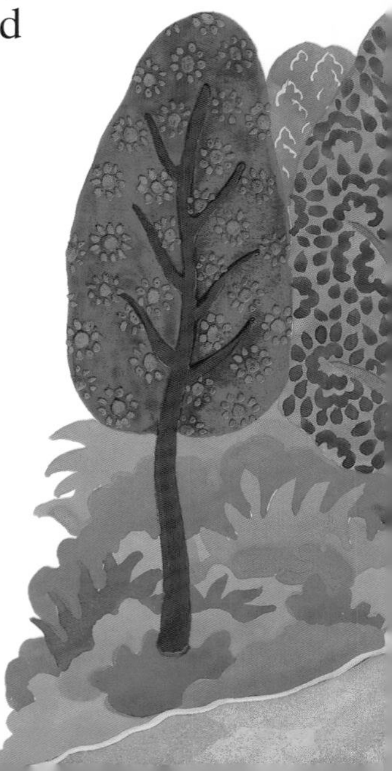

Fortune and wealth deserted the young man, and he went into the forest and was never seen again.

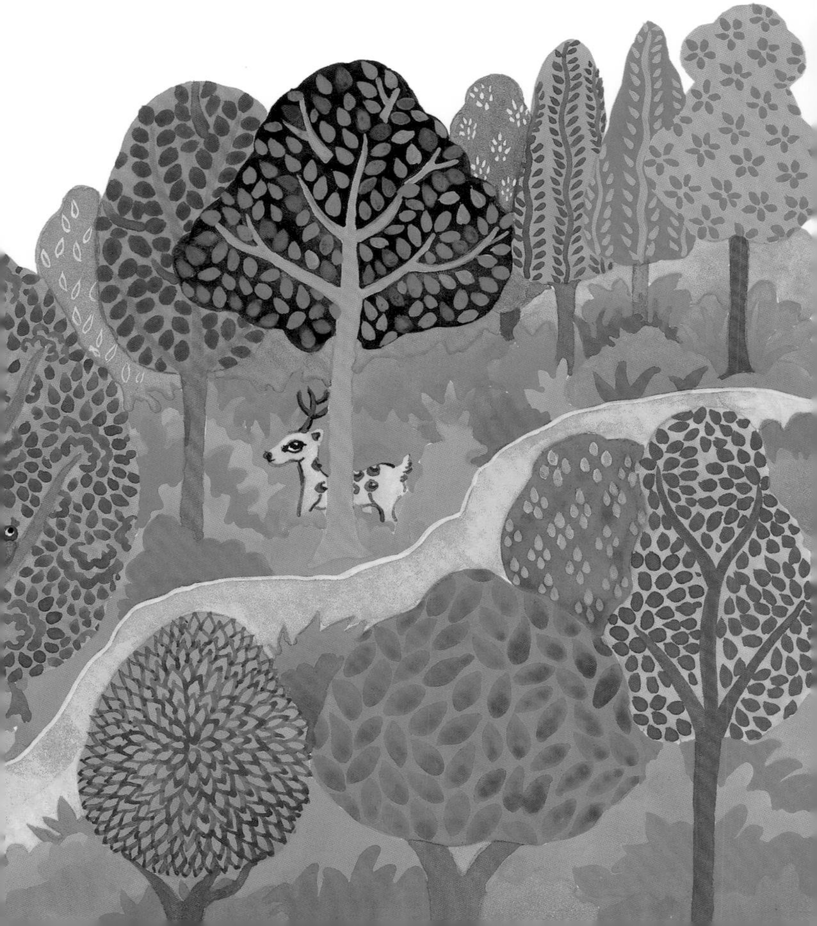